ISAAC O. OLALEYE

IN THE RAINFIELD

Who Is the Greatest?

illustrated by

ANN GRIFALCONI

THE BLUE SKY PRESS
An Imprint of Scholastic Inc. · New York

Dedicated to Ed and Jean Riley,

who opened their home and hearts

to me.

I. O.

To Carl and Pam,

who contributed air and light.

A. G.

THE BLUE SKY PRESS

Text copyright © 2000 by Isaac O. Olaleye

Illustrations copyright © 2000 by Ann Grifalconi

All rights reserved.

For information regarding permission, please write to:

Permissions Department,

The Blue Sky Press, an imprint of Scholastic Inc.,

555 Broadway, New York, New York 10012.

The Blue Sky Press is a registered trademark of Scholastic Inc.

Library of Congress card catalog number: 97-39861

ISBN 0-590-48363-3

10 9 8 7 6 5 4 3 2 1   0/0 01 02 03 04

Printed in Mexico   49

First printing, February 2000

In the Rainfield of the Lingalas tribe of Africa
towered the Mountains of Clouds.
From the Mountains of Clouds,
the River of Birds flowed into
the Land of Giant Apes.

There, in that Rainfield, a very long time ago,
Wind, Fire, and Rain were not good friends
at all. And it happened one day that
they had an argument about
who was the greatest.

"I am the greatest," whistled Wind. "Because I am the fastest of us three. And nobody can see me or catch me. Nobody!"

"I am the greatest," fumed Fire. "Because I am the hottest thing on Earth. And nobody can stand near me. Nobody!"

Rain said softly, "The hottest and the fastest may not be the greatest. The greatest must be the gentlest."

The three bickered back and forth, forth and back. And since they could not agree, they decided to meet in seven days to prove, once and for all, who really was the greatest.

At last the seventh day came.

Wind was first to prove its greatness.

Wind became a gentle breeze, then picked up speed, whistling, *fuuu, fuuu*. Soon its whistling grew into an angry, howling windstorm.

Birds fluttered, flip-flopped, and whimpered, *pinye, pinye,* hurrying back to their nests. Village children huffed and

puffed, *kia kia*, *kata-kiti*, running from the wind. Roofs, huts, and barns flew, *raah raah*, *flap flap*, in the shrieking wind!

Leaves flew.
Fruit flew. Branches
snapped. Trees bent. Goats,
sheep, dogs, and cats floated
in the air. *Meeheheh! Baahah!*
Wow-wow! Meooow! Meow!
Wind! Wind! Wind! Wild wind
everywhere! Everybody prayed for
Wind to stop. Fire and Rain yelled,
"Stop, Wind! Your time is up!"

With one last gust, shrilling Wind stopped. Alas! People were left hanging high in branches when the bent trees straightened. It looked as if farmers, their wives, and their children grew on trees!

Now Fire stepped in and began to crackle, *pere-pere*.
Then Fire fumed with great fury.

Soon a firestorm was eating everything
in its way, *weere, weere*. Animals scrambled
for their burrows, *gara-gara*, and into streams
and rivers, *waka-waka*. People plunged
into lakes and ponds,
yara-yara.

African milk bush whined at the taste of Fire. Kiss-me-quick
plants whined at the taste of Fire. Fire kissed flame
of the forest tree, and the tree
exploded into fountains of fire.

Fire hopped over streams
and lakes and kept on in
a mad rush, going in
every direction.

Fire! Fire! Fire!
Fire power everywhere!
Everybody prayed
for Fire
to stop.

Wind and Rain yelled, "Stop, Fire! Your time is up!"

But Fire fumed, "No! I am the hottest. The hottest is the greatest. The greatest shall not stop!"

Wind blew, *fuuu,fuuu*, trying to snuff out Fire. But that made Fire bigger and stronger! "I cannot stop Fire. Is Fire the greatest?" Wind wondered.

Then, suddenly,
the sky darkened.
Dim! Dimmer!!
Dimmest!!!
Lightning snaked
across the sky.
Thunder rumbled
and roared:
Grr! Grr!
Kaboom!
Kaboom!
Fire crouched,
quivering under
the great cloud
mass. And Rain
began to drip,
gentle even upon
the lowly lily
of the field,
and steadily
upon Fire.

Rain! Rain! Rain!

Singing Rain,

wini-wini, wini-wini,

everywhere!

"I will now stop!"
yelled Fire.
"Too late!"
whistled Wind.
"Too late!"
sang Rain.
A gentle shower
had smothered Fire.
Fire was defeated!

Fire hissed:

"Shunnn! Rain

is the greatest."

And Fire still makes

a hissing noise whenever

water is poured upon it.

Humans and beasts broke forth in cheers for Rain.
And Wind, which could not snuff out Fire,
exclaimed, "Rain is the greatest!"

And to this day, Wind goes round
with Rain, whistling . . .

". . . Rain is the greatest! The gentlest is the greatest!"